Read Me a Story

Text and jacket art by

Rosemary Wells

Interior illustrations by

Jody Wheeler

VOLO

Hyperion Books for Children
New York

 For information address
Hyperion Books for Children, 114 Fifth Avenue,
New York, New York 10011-5690.

Printed in the United States of America

First Edition
1 3 5 7 9 10 8 6 4 2

Library of Congress Cataloging-in-Publication Data
Wells, Rosemary.
Read me a story / text and jacket art by Rosemary Wells; interior illustrations by Jody Wheeler.— 1st ed.
p. cm. — (Yoko & friends— school days)
Summary: Yoko pretends she cannot read because she thinks that if her mother finds out she can, no one will read her a bedtime story.
ISBN 0-7868-0727-X — ISBN 0-7868-1533-7 (pbk.)
[1. Literacy—Fiction. 2. Reading—Fiction. 3. Cats—Fiction. 4. Schools—Fiction. 5. Japanese Americans—Fiction.] I. Wheeler, Jody, ill. II. Title.
PZ7.W46843 Re 2002
[E]—dc21
2001026792

Visit www.hyperionchildrensbooks.com

"It's Alphabet Time, boys and girls," said Mrs. Jenkins.

"It is time for each of us to write our names."

Yoko wrote her name.

Yoko could write everybody else's name too.

She could read the whole first reading book.

But Yoko didn't tell anyone she could read.

She didn't want to.

"Yoko, see if you can read this word," said Mrs. Jenkins.
She wrote CAT
on the blackboard.
"Dog?" asked Yoko.
"No. Let's sound it out," said Mrs. Jenkins.

"Can anyone help Yoko?"

Timothy could help Yoko.

"C-A-T," said Timothy.

"That's very good, Timothy," said Mrs. Jenkins.

The next day Mrs. Jenkins asked

Yoko to read the word PAN.

"Try to sound it out,"

said Mrs. Jenkins.

"Nap?" asked Yoko.

"That's backward," said Grace.

"Grace, why don't you help Yoko?"

said Mrs. Jenkins.

Grace helped Yoko.

The next day at school, Charles helped Yoko sound out the word TOP.

By the end of the week, almost
everyone had helped Yoko.
Her words were CAT, PAN,
TOP, GO, and FAN.

Mrs. Jenkins wrote them

on the board.

"I'm sure Yoko can read them,"

said Mrs. Jenkins.

But Yoko could not read even one.

"I have forgotten them all,"

said Yoko.

Mrs. Jenkins asked Yoko's mother

to come in for a conference.

"Yoko tries really hard,"

said Mrs. Jenkins.

"She is very good at numbers,

drawing, nature, and music.

She knows all her shapes

and all her colors.

She can even write all the letters.

But she is having trouble reading."

Yoko's mother took her to the

doctor to get glasses.

"Yoko has perfect vision," said the

doctor. "She doesn't need glasses."

Mrs. Jenkins was very confused.

She asked Yoko to stay inside at

playtime.

Mrs. Jolly came to give Yoko

a test.

After the test she told Yoko to do reading exercises at home.

Yoko exercised every night for a whole month.

"The exercises don't do any
good," said Yoko's mother
to Mrs. Jenkins.
"Sometimes certain boys and girls
are not ready until they are ready,"
said Mrs. Jenkins.
"I'm not ready," said Yoko.

But on the bus Timothy
whispered to Yoko, "I know
a secret!"

"What?" asked Yoko.

"I saw you write a letter to the
Thunderchip Cornflakes Company.

You sent away for a secret decoder ring. I saw it on the back of their cereal box."

"Oh, I can write just fine," said Yoko.

"How can you write if you can't read?" asked Timothy.

"It's a mystery to me," said Yoko.

Monday morning, Mrs. Jenkins got a letter from the Thunderchip Cornflakes Company.

Dear Teacher (said the letter),

A member of your class, Yoko, has written to us for a secret decoder ring. We would like to offer secret decoder rings to everyone in Hilltop School. They will be only half price.

Yours truly,

George Thunderchip

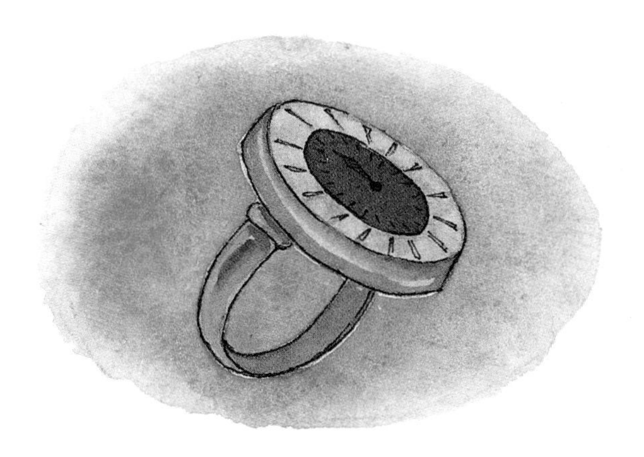

Mrs. Jenkins did not order the decoder rings, but she did call Yoko's mother.

"How can that be?"
asked Yoko's mother.

"How can my daughter write a letter to the Thunderchip Cornflakes Company ordering a secret decoder ring if she is not able to read?"

"She writes beautiful letters," said Mrs. Jenkins. "Let us be thankful for that."

"I am thankful, but I do not understand," said Yoko's mother.

That afternoon Timothy came home to play with Yoko.
"Will you show me how to fold origami paper?" asked Timothy.

"I will teach you how to make a frog," said Yoko.

Yoko made a frog.

"Now let's make stars," said Timothy.

"I don't know how," said Yoko.

"I have never made a star."

Yoko looked at the directions.

"It says, 'Fold paper in half,'" said Yoko. "'Then turn and fold again.'"

"Yoko," said Timothy. "You are reading. You can read better than I can."

"No," said Yoko. "I can't really read. I can only read origami directions."

That night when she had tucked Yoko into bed, Yoko's mother whispered, "Yoko, I think you have a secret."

"No, I don't," said Yoko.

"I overheard you read all the directions," said Yoko's mother.

"That's the only thing I can read," said Yoko.

"Yoko," said her mother. "You are not telling me the whole truth."

"It is a secret," said Yoko, "between me and me."

"I will not ask you to tell your secret, Yoko," said her mother. "But I will ask you why you are keeping it a secret."

"I am afraid," said Yoko.

"Afraid?" asked her mother.

"I am afraid you will stop reading me my story if you know I can read by myself."

"I will never stop reading you your story," said Yoko's mother.

"I will read you a story every single day as long as you want me to.

"But one day a week, maybe you could read a story to me. Do you think you could?"

"I will try," said Yoko.

"Good," said her mother.

"Now it is time for chapter three of *The Green Fairy Book*," said Yoko.

Yoko's mother opened Yoko's favorite book.

Dear Parents,

When our children were young we lived in a small house, but we always made a space just for books. When their dad or I would read a story out loud, the TV was always off—radio and music, too—because it intruded.

Soon this peaceful half hour of every day became like a little island vacation. Our children are lifetime readers now, with an endless curiosity for the rich world waiting between the covers of good books. It cost us nothing but time well spent and a library card.

This set of easy-to-read books is about the real nitty-gritty of elementary school. There are new friends, and bullies, too. There are germs and the "Clean Hands" song, new ways of painting pictures, learning music, telling the truth, gossiping, teasing, laughing, crying, separating from Mama, scary Halloweens, and secret valentines. The stories are all drawn from the experiences my children had in school.

It's my hope that these books will transport you and your children to a setting that's familiar, yet new, a place where you can explore the exciting new world of school together.

Rosemary Wells